ANNE HUTCHINSON'S WAY

JEANNINE ATKINS   Pictures by **MICHAEL DOOLING**

FARRAR STRAUS GIROUX
New York

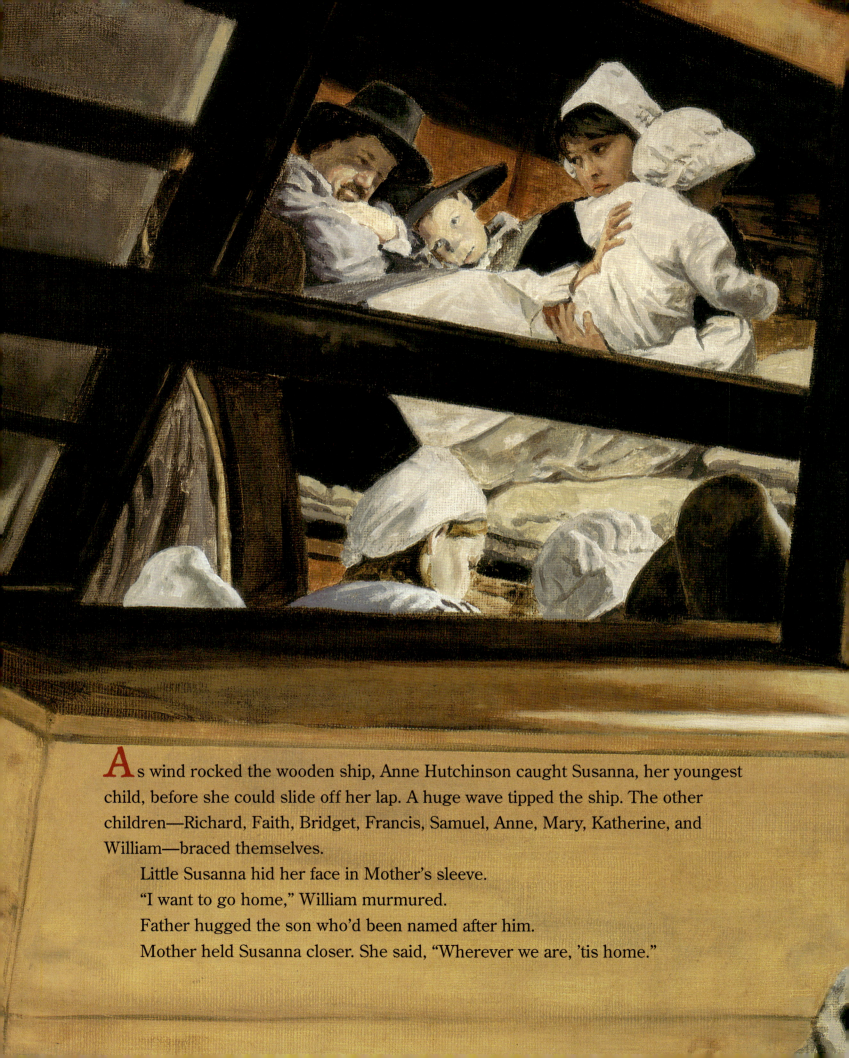

As wind rocked the wooden ship, Anne Hutchinson caught Susanna, her youngest child, before she could slide off her lap. A huge wave tipped the ship. The other children—Richard, Faith, Bridget, Francis, Samuel, Anne, Mary, Katherine, and William—braced themselves.

Little Susanna hid her face in Mother's sleeve.

"I want to go home," William murmured.

Father hugged the son who'd been named after him.

Mother held Susanna closer. She said, "Wherever we are, 'tis home."

The rain stopped by morning. The waves became small again. The minister called the passengers together for a long sermon.

The ship's passengers were all Puritans, people who wanted to reform, or "purify," the Church of England. When King Charles punished some Puritans for finding fault with their country's church, the Hutchinson family decided to leave England. They joined other Puritans crossing the Atlantic to live where they could worship more simply, without the bowing, kneeling, statues, and stained glass windows that they felt came between them and the Almighty.

As everyone gathered, the minister said, "The Lord sends storms to punish the wicked among us."

"This minister speaks too much of storms," Mother said. "In the New World we hope to spend more time giving thanks for the blessings of blue skies. We are not going there to be frightened again."

On September 18, 1634, after sixty-two days at sea, the ship reached the
Massachusetts Bay Colony, which had been founded a few years before. Susanna
was carried onto the Boston shore. She waited for her turn to hug her oldest
brother, Edward, who'd left England earlier with their uncle. She saw the minister
from the ship speaking to some men. They seemed to frown at Mother.

"Come see the house that Uncle and I built for us," Edward said. He clasped
Susanna's hand and led the family past the marketplace, the meetinghouse, and a
jail, to a big house. He said, "'Tis across from Governor Winthrop's home."

During the following days, the family settled into their new home, which smelled of fresh wood and straw from the thatched roof. Susanna's sisters helped Father unpack cloth for his fabric shop.

On the Sabbath, the girls put on their best dresses, then went to the meetinghouse. They wiggled close to Mother, while Father and the boys crowded a bench across the room. The minister spoke with a rough, yelling voice, the sort that Mother did not allow at home.

Governor Winthrop's wife invited the family to visit. Susanna was shy around the Winthrops' four boys and big dogs. Her brothers liked the boys, but said the governor and his wife forbade much talking and laughing.

When Samuel returned from the Winthrop house one day, he said, "We counted fourteen guns on the wall."

"I suppose 'tis the governor's means of keeping the colony safe," Mother said. "I don't see that we have much to fear, though."

The evenings grew colder, and Father made bigger fires. One night when snow was falling, Susanna heard a knock. Mother grabbed a lantern and hurried outside. As wolves howled in the woods, she looked back at the house.

"Mother says babies come even in the middle of the night," said Mary. "She wants to be there to greet them."

When Mother delivered babies, she met women who were too busy to get to morning-long sermons. She asked them to come hear her talk about Scripture, which, as a minister's daughter, she'd done for much of her life. Every Monday evening, she set candles in the windows. She sent the youngest children to bed, but Susanna heard scraping benches and rustling cloaks and peeked through cracks in the floorboards.

"Children may forget their manners or quarrel, but their parents never stop loving them," Mother said. "Surely the Lord is even more forgiving."

At last spring arrived and the hills turned green. A neighbor gave the
Hutchinsons a puppy. Edward married a young woman he'd known in England. Faith,
Susanna's oldest sister, married a tailor who came to Father's shop for cloth.

Two aunts moved in and helped in the kitchen. They showed Susanna where to
pick blueberries. They gathered wee chamomile flowers, which Mother used to cure
headaches, and wild mint for soothing stomachs.

Susanna liked the hills more than the marketplace, where she turned her eyes from the stocks and the whipping post. Samuel said, "The Winthrop boys told us a man was whipped for kissing his wife right in front of everyone. A thief had his hand cut off, truly. Someone was banished—he was sent from his home!—because he said the minister was dull."

Susanna covered her ears.

In the fall, birds left the sky. The second winter wasn't quite as cold as the first. Father built a cradle, and in March of 1636 Mother put a baby in it. "Do you want to hold Zuriel?" she asked.

Susanna held out her arms for the new baby in the New World.

Susanna played tag with William, Mary, and the two youngest Winthrop boys. One said that their father had caught a man taking firewood from the stack by the door, and let him keep the logs. Susanna was glad.

By the time baby Zuriel was a year old and learning to walk, Mother had begun holding meetings on Thursday nights, when men joined the women, as well as on Mondays. The men smelled of the fish they caught or the shoes they mended or the wood they chopped. Not everyone fit in the common room. Some leaned in the open windows and jammed the doorway.

As the meetings grew more crowded, people who did not attend whispered that it was wrong for a woman to preach. Father's shop became less busy.

One night a rock broke a window.

Faith and her husband came the next morning. "Mother, you are putting the whole family in danger!" she said. "You must stop your talks. 'Tis best for all to listen and obey the minister."

"The Lord blessed us with minds to use and mouths to speak what we see as truth," Mother said.

In November 1637, the colony leaders ordered Anne Hutchinson to stop her meetings. Mother refused, and was charged with breaking the peace of the Massachusetts Bay Colony.

On the morning that Mother left for court, she gave ten kisses—one to each child. Mary slipped Mother's cloak over her shoulders. William tried to look brave. Susanna tugged on Mother's sleeves, which smelled of chamomile and mint.

"Be strong," Mother said. "Pray for me."

Susanna closed her eyes to pray. She remembered that Governor Winthrop had let the man who'd stolen firewood keep it. Wouldn't he be kind?

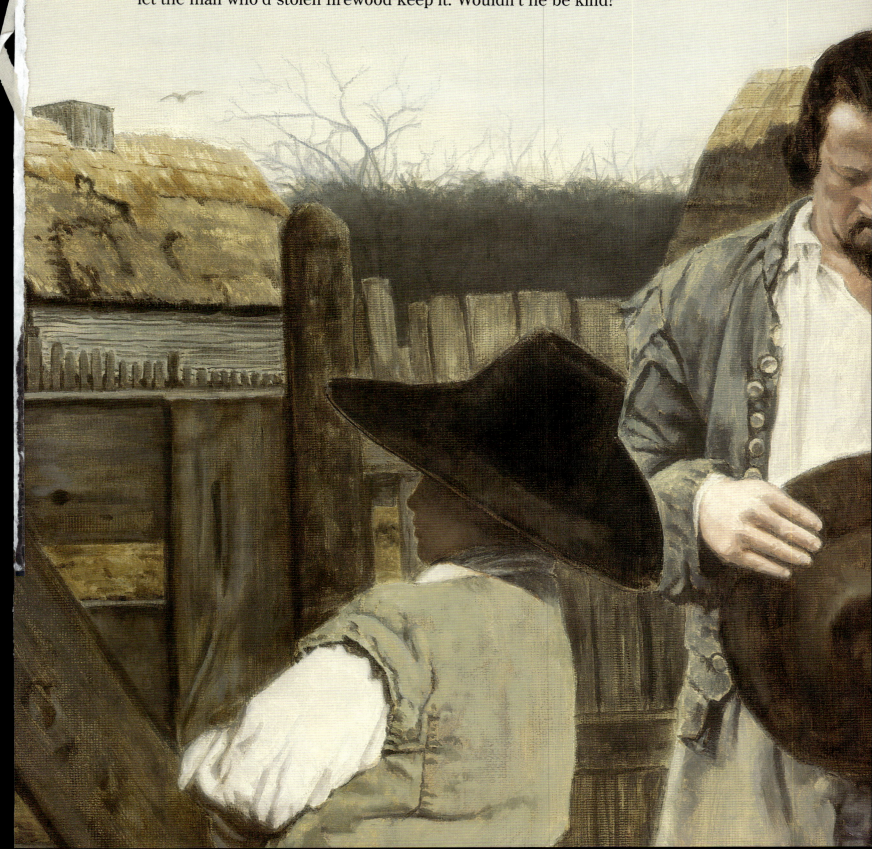

At night Mother and Father came home. Father said, "The governor sat among forty-eight men who claim your mother disturbs the peace because her beliefs differ from the minister's. They say it is against the law for a woman to hold meetings."

"I speak in our home, where 'tis my duty to teach my children right from wrong, and I will not close our doors to neighbors," Mother said. "The colony leaders want another day to decide how I will be punished."

"Mother, can't you stop your talks?" Susanna said.

"Holding one's tongue is a good way to sell cloth," Father said. "But 'tis not your mother's way. Keeping her beliefs to herself would be like keeping food from the hungry or medicine from people in pain."

In the morning, Mother prepared to return to court. Susanna clung to her. Father had to pry away Susanna's hands. She cried when Mother left, even though her sisters kissed her wrists and fingertips.

Susanna and William counted forty-nine stones, which they pretended were the lawmakers, the minister, and the governor. They found a big, pretty stone to stand for Mother and kicked all but that stone.

At night, Susanna was the first to greet Father. He said, "Governor Winthrop ordered your mother to leave the Massachusetts Bay Colony. He knows the wilderness is too cold and snowy for our family to cross now, but Mother cannot come home. Since the prison is for men, she must spend the winter locked in one room in a house across the river."

Susanna's aunts and older sisters took over Mother's household work. They cooked, scrubbed pots, mended dresses, and cleaned candlesticks. Just before dark, Bridget counted the children's heads. Bridget was a good big sister, but when she baked, she forgot to dab vanilla behind Susanna's ears.

In January of 1638, Father and some friends made plans to look for land to settle. "I cannot take you with us. If it storms, finding a safe place in the woods will be easier with just a few men and a dog," he told the children. "We'll build houses and send back a map so you and Mother can come in spring."

That winter was unusually cold. Susanna couldn't see through the frost on the windows. When neighbors ran out of firewood, they burned benches in their hearths. Richard and Bridget studied the carved chest they had brought from England and talked about which they needed more, furniture or firewood.

Susanna's older sisters and brothers visited Mother. They told Susanna about the bolt on Mother's door.

"I want to see her!" Susanna cried.

"You're too little for the two-mile journey," Bridget said. She looked out at snow that was piled as high as Susanna's shoulders.

At last ice broke on the bay, and Mother came home. Her hands didn't smell of chamomile and mint. Her pale face was thin. She said, " 'Tis time to leave Massachusetts and join your father."

Mother, Richard, Bridget, Francis, Samuel, Anne, Mary, Katherine, William, Susanna, and Zuriel set out with two other families and their dogs. Across the road, the four Winthrop boys peered from a window. Women came to their doors holding the babies Mother had helped bring into the world. From the top of a hill, Susanna looked back at the house where they had lived for three and a half years.

Every day they walked about nine miles, following Father's map. They met people who lent them canoes to ride across rivers. Susanna's feet hurt, but she didn't complain.

At last they reached a deep, wide waterway. They climbed into a boat. Cold waves smacked the sides as they rowed to an island.

Susanna heard hammers, saws, and the barking of their dog.

"Welcome!" Father shouted.

Surely here there was room for people who were brave, those who were afraid, and those who were sometimes both. Susanna stepped onto the shore and reached back for her little brother. "We are here," she said. "We are home."

Afterword

This fictionalized story is based on the real Hutchinson family, who settled on an island in Narragansett Bay. They were joined by about sixty more people who sought freedom of religion and speech. The Hutchinsons had lived there nearly four years when Susanna's father died in 1642. Hearing rumors that this region of Rhode Island might become part of Massachusetts, Anne Hutchinson decided to head farther south, where she wouldn't be subject to Massachusetts law. She and her six youngest children traveled to the Dutch colony of New Netherland. They built a house in what is now the borough of the Bronx in New York City.

Anne Hutchinson knew there was fighting between Dutch settlers and the Algonquian-speaking Indians, who were angry that some of their land was being settled without permission or payment. Anne Hutchinson hoped to be friends with everyone. She refused to own a gun.

In August of 1643, Susanna was picking berries when Indians killed her mother, sisters, and brothers. They kidnapped Susanna and cared for her for several years. When her release became part of a peace treaty between the Indians and the settlers, Susanna was reluctant to leave. She returned to Boston to live with her brother Edward, his wife, and their children, including a baby they'd named Anne. In 1651, Susanna married. She gave birth to eleven children. She taught them about her mother, whose words, faith, and courage would never be forgotten.

The Hutchinson River, which flows through southeastern New York into Long Island Sound, was named after the woman who was ordered to be silent, but dared to speak out. Boston, Massachusetts, which once banished Anne Hutchinson (1591–1643), now honors her with a statue outside the State House. This monument shows a strong woman looking up, her hand resting on her daughter's shoulder.

To Susan Wisner Weeks
—J.A.
For Jane, as always
—M.D.

The artist gratefully acknowledges Susan Wilkinson of Historic St. Mary's City in Maryland
for sharing her knowledge of period clothing.

Text copyright © 2007 by Jeannine Atkins
Illustrations copyright © 2007 by Michael Dooling
All rights reserved
Distributed in Canada by Douglas & McIntyre Ltd.
Color separations by Chroma Graphics PTE Ltd.
Printed and bound in the United States of America by Phoenix Color Corporation
Designed by Barbara Grzeslo
First edition, 2007
1 3 5 7 9 10 8 6 4 2

www.fsgkidsbooks.com